Hammer, hammer. Bang, bang. Scooby-Doo, Shaggy, and their friends were building a playground.

Daphne's uncle gave the neighborhood
supplies to build a new playground.
The gang was helping out.
Shaggy banged at a nail.
"Oops!" Shaggy said to Scooby.
"Almost nailed you instead."

By Gail Herman

Illustrated by Duendes

SCHOLASTIC INC.
New York   Toronto   London   Auckland   Sydney
Mexico City   New Delhi   Hong Kong

ISBN 0-439-16169-X

25 24 23 22 21   8 9 10 11 12 13 14/0

Designed by Mary Hall
Printed in the U.S.A.
First Scholastic printing, May 2000

"Stop all this noise!" an old woman shouted. She rushed out from the house next door, and frowned at the gang. "What is going on here?"

"We are building a playground," Drew
Zooka said. He was the person in charge.
The woman scowled.

"Playgrounds are noisy! I don't want one here. I'll find a way to stop it. Or my name is not Edna Spring."

The next morning, the gang came back to work.

"We're not letting Edna Spring stop us!" said Drew.

"We need to start on the sandbox," he told the gang.

"Did someone say lunch box?"
Shaggy asked.

"Let's take a lunch break," Shaggy
told Scooby.

"Lunch?" said Drew. "But it's nine o'clock! And we have work to do!"

"No you don't!" Edna Spring walked up to the gang. "I'd stop building if I were you!"

"I know, I know." Drew Zooka sighed. "You don't want a playground here."

The old woman shook her head. "That's not it. Werewolves are haunting this place. I heard howling all night long. This is not the place for a playground."

"Werewolves?" Daphne asked.

"This sounds like a case for Mystery, Inc.!" Fred said.

"There is one way to find out about these werewolves," Velma said.

"There's a full moon tonight," Fred told the gang.

"We'll stay in the park tonight," Velma added. "And see if any werewolves come."

That night, the full moon rose over the park. Piles of wood cast strange shadows, and Shaggy felt scared. He waited a moment, but all was quiet.

"There's nothing going on here!" he said. "Scoob, let's grab a late night snack and go home!"

"Reah!" Scooby agreed.

"Not so fast!" said Velma.

"Would you stay for a Scooby Snack?"
Daphne asked.

In a flash, Shaggy and Scooby gulped the
treats.

"Still hungry!" said Shaggy. "Time to go!"

Awhooo! A howl echoed through the park.

"Is that your stomach grumbling, good buddy?" asked Shaggy.

Scooby shook his head. "Rope!"

Shaggy gulped. "Then it's the werewolves!" he cried.

Shaggy and Scooby jumped in fright.
They raced to the gate.
"Like I've had enough playtime
at this playground!" said Shaggy.
But a howling sound came from the gate.
"Rerewolf!" Scooby cried.

Scooby and Shaggy ran, with the werewolf right behind.

They raced around the swings.

"Ouch!" said Shaggy as one of the swings hit him in the head.

Aaa-oooooh! the werewolf howled.

Shaggy and Scooby raced up the slide, then slid down.

They couldn't get away!

"Scooby! Shaggy!" Velma called. "Stop playing around!"

"Velma!" Shaggy cried. "Help!"

"Relp!" Scooby barked.

Shaggy saw a pile of sandbags for the sandbox.

"We can jump onto those," he told Scooby.

Scooby squeezed his eyes shut. "Rone," he counted. "Roo, ree."

"Jump!" shouted Shaggy.

They jumped onto the bags — and heard another howl.

"Like, it's the werewolf again!" Shaggy shouted.

But Scooby shook his head. Now that he was closer, he knew it wasn't a werewolf. It was more like . . .

"Ruppies!" he said.

"Puppies?" asked Shaggy.

Scooby nudged the bags. And there were four puppies, waiting to play.

Shaggy said, "Well, okay, Scoob.
You found some puppies. But what about
those werewolves?"

"Those *are* the werewolves," Velma said, walking up behind them.

"Don't you see?" Fred said. "They are howling because they are cold and hungry."

"More noise!" Edna Spring interrupted.
"Yes," said Drew Zooka, hurrying over.
"I came to check on things here. What's
going on?"

Scooby found the werewolves," Velma explained.

Drew looked very surprised.

"But they're only puppies!" Daphne added.

"Puppies!" said Edna. "How sweet!"

"Redna's ruppies," Scooby said.

"Great idea!" said Velma.

"Edna, would you like to give these puppies a home?" Fred asked.

Edna smiled. "Would I ever! And you know what? A playground is a great place for puppies to play."

One week later, the playground was finished. Right in the middle stood a statue of Scooby and the puppies.

"I've named the puppies Daphne, Fred, Velma, and Shaggy," Edna told everyone. "Not Scooby?" asked Velma.

"There's only one Scooby-Doo!" Edna said.
"Scooby-Dooby-Doo!" Scooby howled.